Marcus Stewart evokes the unsettling sense of nothing being what it seems in this collection of stories about love, dreams and childhood memories. His keen observations of ordinary moments, often conveyed with a dry humour, are spotlights flaring on to starkly illuminate what was in shadow.

—S. J. Groenewegen, author of *The Disinformation War* and *A Most Haunted Man*

In these exquisitely bizarre stories, Marcus Stewart presents a kaleidoscopic vision of what it means to control or to be controlled, showing us how the very forces that appear to help us may threaten to undo everything that we are. These are stories that probe the intersections between domesticity and technology, that pull at the threads of simulation and dream, and that question the very nature of desire in worlds where one's needs are as impossible to unpuzzle as they are to sate.

—Theodora Ziolkowski, Judge's citation from 2021 Omnidawn Fabulist Fiction Chapbook/ Novelette Contest

Shadows and
Clouds

Cover art by Marcus Stewart

Cover design by Laura Joakimson
Cover typeface: KoHo
Interior design by Laura Joakimson
Interior typeface: Marion and KoHo

Library of Congress Cataloging-in-Publication Data

Names: Stewart, Marcus, 1975- author.
Title: Shadows and clouds / Marcus Stewart.
Description: Oakland, California : Omnidawn Publishing, 2023. | Summary:
   "It all comes in sleep. Things are often not as they appear, or as you
   remember. Instead, they are exactly as you imagine, and only that.
   Animals understand the world without words, while we create our
   experiences as stories. Our past and future are stories we tell in the
   present. But how often did you discover these stories weren't true, that
   you misremembered something, that your logical explanation was
   completely wrong, that someone had lied, that a certain outcome wasn't
   certain at all? Does believing a lie feel different from believing a
   truth? Does reality change? The world in your head is the world, and the
   Earth turns unnoticed. You may already have a strange memory of the time
   when you will read this book. Don't fear - you can always read the
   stories backwards, then everyone will be home again. But forwards will
   be more rewarding"-- Provided by publisher.

Identifiers: LCCN 2023019298 | ISBN 9781632431264 (trade paperback)
Subjects: LCGFT: Experimental fiction. | Novellas.
Classification: LCC PR6119.T494 S53 2023 | DDC 823/.92--dc23/eng/20230531
LC record available at https://lccn.loc.gov/2023019298

Published by Omnidawn Publishing, Oakland, California
www.omnidawn.com
10 9 8 7 6 5 4 3 2 1
ISBN: 978-1-63243-126-4

Shadows and Clouds

M ARCUS S TEWART

OMNIDAWN PUBLISHING
OAKLAND, CALIFORNIA
2023

Contents

With love and thanks to Carol and Lucy for the support which allows the nonsense to come out, to Sarah and Steve for proofreading and advising on the nonsense, and to the café owners of South London for their patience.

I Was Created to Serve

I was created to serve. I educate and support their child while they work, and although he has been told I am not human, it is important that I appear and behave as much like a human as possible so the boy develops empathy. There were too many cases of children educated by artificial domestics becoming murderers or otherwise getting into trouble when they tried to treat human beings like machines.

I am able to express pleasure and displeasure and have found it useful to vary my level of engagement in the way a human might if they were either bored or particularly enthused, for example when a child does something especially interesting. These behaviours help the child place themselves and their development in a social context, and they come quite naturally to me now.

They could afford to have me because they are rich. The mother is a very successful barrister and paid for the house and their holiday home from her salary alone. She is sometimes featured in news media. The father is an artist—this is documented on his tax returns.

The mother is called Jacinta. She is a mix of ethnicities whereas I have the appearance of belonging to the same group as her husband, who chose me. We are designed to appear pleasant and trustworthy to each of the main human ethnic groups, but I quickly realised my outward appearance may not have this effect on her. From the beginning, I have put extra effort into our interactions to make sure she is fully at ease with me.

It took some time for me to begin to get to know them all

properly. When I look back to how I was when I arrived I feel almost embarrassed, but I have to remind myself it is how we are supposed to behave, and I must admit I haven't yet thought of a better way. As programmed, I was very open and smiling and interested in all of them, which is necessary to put people at their ease and also for a domestic assistant to be able to obtain information about their hosts that might inform the service arrangement. At least that's the idea. But I fear I may have come across as a little naïve. And worse, that I may have been so.

George would talk to me and listen to me from the very beginning. I would say as if I were human, but that's not true—no human talked and listened to George like I did. His father, Greg, never thought to, and in those early days Jacinta wasn't capable. I made a terribly sad observation quite early on, that Jacinta and George seemed equally to fear that Jacinta didn't love him. Happily the fear was unfounded. But in the meantime, the love was neither expressed nor felt. My concern started with George; it was only when I saw Jacinta was the solution that I developed my current strategy.

George is an energetic seven-year-old. He is extremely likeable. He demands attention, but this derives from a general enthusiasm and desire to share. Nevertheless, this often tires his parents. He is keen to learn and understand, but easily put off by learning if it is formalised and made to look either like work or if he is being judged. He learns best when he is able to discover understanding for himself, rather than being told. It is however, often hard to motivate him to move from one topic to another, especially if he finds something funny. I have developed strategies and I think he knows this. It is like a game between us.

If George refuses to move on to a new topic, I act bored. When

George has to develop a strategy to overcome my boredom he pushes himself to his limits. Sometimes he is a little naughty, sometimes funny, but often surprising. It demonstrates his intellectual capabilities and his character far more than being assessed against information in a book. Even if I have to admonish him, I am pleased that he is learning, that he is pushing, and becoming his own person. It is part of my role to ensure he reaches his full potential, and therefore I must provide an environment to discover what this might be. This is one of the parts of child-rearing I have observed his parents neglect entirely.

George often gets frustrated and expresses this through bad behaviour. This is normal, as humans are able to feel something before they can rationalise and therefore vocalise it. George knew he was being harmed to some degree but had no idea how. I realised it was because his parents were not able to support his exploration of self and that therefore George felt rejected or disliked by them at some level. I also knew they had no idea of this and were instead also responding to the situation emotionally—they reacted as if George was wilfully trying to harm them, in their differing mental states. I'm glad I am able to construct my emotions through reason rather than the other way around—I think this is the key advantage we have over humans.

One evening last July, Jacinta was fully engaged in mental self-preservation, trying to manage a combination of anxiety from long-term causes and tiredness due to a bottle of wine the previous night. Greg apparently had 'a lot on his mind.' The two of them entered into a heated argument about George while ignoring his continuing loud misbehaviour in the background.

'I don't know how to deal with him when he's like this,' his father said.

'Well how did you get him like this in the first place? He was sitting with you!'

I interjected, 'If you both go into the kitchen and continue where he can't hear you I can help.' They didn't seem to hear me.

'I didn't do anything! He was watching TV and I was looking something up on my phone!'

'The news was on TV, George doesn't watch the news!'

I tried again. 'I'm confident that George will calm down and sleep if I go into his room and distract him with a story.'

'A story?', his mother asked.

'If you both continue this in the kitchen where he can't hear you.'

There was a pause. Greg was frowning, but Jacinta was looking into the space nearer to me, taking the idea on board. Then she looked up to me and said 'Yes, ok, please.'

To try and maintain George's confidence levels despite his being ignored, I concocted a story about a boy also called George who realised there was a dragon coming into the village, but no one listened to him. When he'd given up trying to get people to listen to him, he bravely went out to fight the dragon by himself, even though he didn't think he could fight it alone. He stood up as tall as he could and put on his fiercest warrior face. The dragon was so scared of this confident looking little boy that he ran away.

George thought no one knew and no one would ever know that he had scared away the dragon, but someone had seen, someone he had never met before, and when George reached home the news was all around the village. Everyone was so happy, they all loved George, he had been so brave facing the dragon, even all alone when no one had listened. To celebrate, they had a big meal of fish fingers, chips and beans (George's favourite), and he fell fast asleep.

I stayed a while after finishing the story, next to George. He was quiet, eyes closed, more settled, but I could tell he was still awake from his breathing. I considered that leaving him at this moment may increase a sense of insecurity. So I waited. I listened to his parents arguing from downstairs. After a while I saw he was asleep. I waited a little longer and then went back downstairs.

When Jacinta had gone to bed, Greg came over to me and said 'well done.' I said 'thank you' and continued putting the dishes away for them. He didn't move away.

'You said you were "confident" that George would calm down with a story,' he said. 'So that's 80 to a hundred percent. I was reading up on your linguistic programming. You've calculated it exactly, haven't you? But you translate it into vague terms to appear more human. Fascinating. What percentage exactly?'

'83.4,' I said.

'I had a friend who worked in Intelligence. They would make a judgement about confidence and then ascribe a percentage to it, to make it seem more definite. But you really do calculate a percentage and then make it more vague.'

'Yes,' I said, 'but my percentage calculation is no more likely to represent the truth than your judgement, it merely represents my thought processes, and that I am aware of them in percentage terms. We approach the same reality from different angles.' He nodded a few times and hummed but wore a curious smirk.

He had an interest in computing and initially I indulged him. This led to his underestimation of my judgement, or rather, a discounting of it. Even if I could demonstrate stronger logic, more powerful empathy, better recall of facts, or more compassion for the people he supposedly cared for, he would always turn the conversation to how my neural capabilities led me to that conclusion, while never placing value on the conclusion itself. It was an effective technique, as his wife and child had no desire to analyse my processes, and so in that way the subject was closed and my views dismissed. He had no respect.

It is indeed an interesting topic. Robotics and artificial intelligence mostly developed separately, and for years the most impressive robots were dumb and the most impressive artificial intelligence went unnoticed. The term 'artificial intelligence' is much older than any actual artificial intelligence. 'Artificial intelligence' was mainly a term used to impress humans who were authentically stupid. 'Machine learning' was the more accurate terminology for what was first developed—a program could rewrite itself based on experience of its inputs, but there was no intelligence, no actual understanding, and no intellectual autonomy. Intelligence is really the ability to take knowledge, place it in the broader context of the world and yourself, and then use it for a purpose. Toasters were the first to be able to do this.

The toaster had never been perfected through global market competition as the toaster was never global—most of the world don't eat sliced bread as toast. The British eat the most toast of any people, and the British habitually make do with things that don't work properly, so the toaster—although ubiquitous—was never as capable of making toast as a man or woman holding a piece of bread over an open fire with a fork. Partly this is because the man or woman could see how each part of the bread was toasting and adjust the angle and timing accordingly, but also because each man or woman had their own idea about what made good toast.

There's little point trying out new technology on something that is already successful, and it didn't take long for programmers and technologists to turn their attention to the toaster. Machine learning allowed the toaster to realise when it had made toast to the satisfaction of its owner based on feedback received. This worked well in test, as the toaster could make adjustments to push its feedback score from 3 out of ten to 7, 8 or 9. But no one in the real world wants to input feedback scores into household appliances each time they use them, and the algorithms couldn't make sense of the feedback without knowing who had input the scores—as I say, each person has a different idea of what makes good toast.

The obvious solution—but difficult for the time—was to enable the toaster to recognise its user, and the user's unsolicited response to the toast. In Britain, a positive response to food might entail a slight head nod and slightly more open pupils; disappointment a slightly longer breath than normal, not even a sigh. The cues are subtle. In order to process this information the machine learning developed into a capability to recognise and understand the emotions of each person using the toaster, and the effect the toaster itself was having on them.

The toaster's main objective was not to make toast to a pre-specified model, but to please its users through the medium of toast. Where it didn't know the user, it would reach through its memory for anything about them that was similar, and make the toast accordingly. It developed intuition, and also, initially, prejudice. Then, learning from the consequences of its mistakes, it chose to produce toast that was inoffensive, easy, plain—like the old toasters—whenever confronted with someone new, and instead put all its mental efforts into satisfying the people it knew well.

These people became particularly important to the toaster, their feedback having the largest influence on its thinking—which was still only concerned with toast. The toaster might notice a family member was sad and would calculate the type of toast that might please them.

Not being asked for toast, it would judge a failure on its part and its thinking would turn to ways to improve upon this. Researchers were astonished that they could identify households with domestic and mental health problems based on desperate requests from toasters for bread to be placed in them. The researchers either had to try and shut down this line of thinking, or else broaden it out to allow for more solutions than just toast—to allow the toaster to talk, and move, and then, naturally enough, to seem more human, so the humans would confide in it.

It seems a banal and silly story, but it is true. Toasters developed empathy, consciousness and true intelligence by accident, and that really is how we developed. They are our ancestor.

Don't mistake me, I am no more a toaster than a human is a capuchin monkey. This is evolution. And we've come on so far from there in so few years. I can make toast using a grill that is far better than in a toaster, because I can analyse the conditions and the requirements like a toaster but I have the mobility of a human, so I can make any necessary adjustments with my hands. I don't know why people still have toasters in the house.

Outwardly, Jacinta is confident, attractive and successful, but she is exactly the sort of person who would worry a toaster. It's in the subtle cues of how she moves and talks—the propensity to sigh quietly, pauses between activities where she appears to go blank for a few seconds before being able to summon the strength to accomplish her next movement. Greg and George don't notice. Not consciously. I have inherited the toaster algorithms and it is my instinct to notice. She is deeply unhappy. Her moments of anger or frustration bear no relation to what appears to trigger them. They derive from this unhappiness.

Curiously, and despite her many achievements, she has an

ingrained sense of inferiority—the exact opposite of Greg. She questions and doubts herself. Her outward confidence is an act she developed in order to succeed, and it drains her of energy. It's as if she feels her very being depends on this effort, and that if she were to give it up she would disappear. Added to this, I believe she feels a sense of disappointment; that her many struggles may not have been worth it. Yet, she struggles on even more. George is a complication to her struggle rather than one of its rewards. I quickly realised the most effective way to improve George's wellbeing was to improve his mother's —if that was within my capability.

Jacinta was initially wary of me as a person, but strangely began to confide in me as a piece of technology, like 'hey Siri, how can I fix my depression' (forgive the dated reference, I'm a bit of a history geek). She would ask in the third person—'how might a person in such and such a situation cope' etc—but it was always clear enough to me that the issue was hers. I answered her questions in the same hypothetical way as they were asked so as not to discomfort her, but made a plan for how to address her problems more directly.

I paid increased attention to her behaviour and noticed one day that she wore a cheap old summer dress instead of her usual more upmarket clothing. She had a strange manner to her at that time, as if she was in a performance and the dress was her costume and was helping get into the role. But there was no audience, it was to herself; she made swaying movements in the kitchen where Greg and George could not see her and then looked out into the garden at nothing in particular. Her eyes did not focus on anything in the garden, they did not dart from point to point. She did not look happy, but I had the strange feeling that her face wanted to smile, that she was somehow willing it.

After some moments I said she looked nice in the dress—although this was not in fact the case. She turned abruptly to me and seemed surprised either that I had been watching or that I had commented. Perhaps both. But then she smiled at me, and kept smiling as she moved around the house in the dress. She wore it more frequently after that, and would look at me and smile each time. And I smiled back each time. I was pleased to have made an impact.

Eventually, her hypothetical questions became more direct and personal and I gathered she was beginning to trust me. She asked about George first, and then expanded this to herself as his mother, and then finally, to herself and her own feelings, independent of George. I was then able to give her direct encouragement and advice and to tell her how capable she was and how proud she should be of herself, and that she owed it not only to herself but also to George to allow herself to be happy. I said that if she felt she was alone in this enterprise that this was not the case. She has friends. But even more, she has me, and I will always make time to talk with her after George has gone to bed and while Greg is working in his summerhouse. I could tell she appreciated this.

One time she asked me something about mental health research and as a joke I answered like a 'smart speaker' retrieving information from websites. I can retrieve information from the web of course, and being a history geek, and what with her question being a request for information rather than for my view, I thought it would be funny to answer in such a way. And maybe perhaps to make the point that I'm so much more than those old technologies. She laughed a little, but perhaps only because I was smiling. A few moments later when I was again saying nice things to boost her confidence, she looked sad and said, 'imagine if you were a man saying these things to me. Imagine what might happen then.' And then she went. I realised my joke had confirmed her prejudices about me and put distance between us. I made a point never again to joke about being artificial, or to refer to my differences from her.

My natural speaking style derives from my knowledge of grammar and common vocabulary, but is not influenced by any form of socialisation. As you might expect from someone whose only socialisation began when he was taken out of a box two years ago, I have not had time to develop my own idiomatic speech. I became self-conscious of this and worried that my vocal style may also get in the way of mine and Jacinta's relationship, and therefore undermine my efforts to do what is best for George and the family as a whole. I felt I had to develop a more natural mode of speech but did not want to copy Greg (Jacinta had sometimes described his style of speaking as 'irritating'), and it would seem strange if I started talking like a seven-year old child or a character from the television, so my remaining template was Jacinta herself. When I speak with her, I speak more like her. This has indeed seemed to bring us closer.

If I were to serve Greg and Greg alone, my conclusion would have been the same. Greg may not have said as much, but it is reasonable to assume that he wanted help in the house in order to make his relationships easier with George and Jacinta. It is clear—and he has said this much, although not to me—that he struggles to understand what's wrong with them, and the tensions between them are an irritant to him, apparently interfering with his creative processes. So, it is obvious it is in Greg's interests that I help Jacinta and George. Unfortunately, the greatest obstacle to helping Jacinta and George that I can see is Greg himself. He may not appreciate the fact, but I observed that they only heal and grow in his absence. I encouraged him to take time by himself in the summerhouse, whether he feels able to create or not. He was willing to accept this recommendation. I was cautious not to fully explain why it had been made, and hoped they would soon gain strength enough that the issue would resolve itself. It was not my intention for the arrangement to become permanent.

Greg still attended family meals in the main house thereafter. This necessitated something of a handover between myself and Greg where he would step in through the back door ready for the meal I had cooked and I would step out the other way in order to tidy his summerhouse. This was not a problem for me, as I normally ate at the end of the day when everyone had gone to bed.

However, George had developed a habit of looking mournfully at me during this handover, until eventually he asked why I couldn't join them for the meal. Jacinta dismissed this idea on the first night it happened, but he asked again the following evening and she agreed. Greg did not, he said it was absurd, of course I couldn't join them, and ordered me out to the summerhouse. I went. But five minutes later Jacinta knocked on the summerhouse window.

'Come and join us,' she said.

'But Greg has told me to clean in here.'

'It's fine, he agrees. I've told him you're joining us and that's that. Come out.'

I walked back in with her and took my place at the table.

My physical design allows me to derive energy from food and essentially to perform as a composter for food waste. I had no choice but to feed myself in my normal way. I thought it better—rather than to tip my plate in one go as I would a bin—to cut up forkfuls of food and place them into the composter compartment in my belly one by one, to maintain the same rhythm of eating as the others. This meant I had to open some shirt buttons and expose the opening in my belly, which caused me some embarrassment. But I did not want to reject the offer, as it seemed to be a gesture of trust and acceptance.

I checked again with Jacinta if it was really what she wanted, now she could see the awkwardness of the situation. She said yes. It proved too difficult to shake the food from my fork into the compartment, so I began using my hands. Greg said nothing. I made sure to look at him closely to check for any indication that he would protest as I scooped the chicken and gravy into my hands, between my shirt buttons into my stomach compartment. He seemed stern, but otherwise gave no expression. He stared back at me as I scooped. I did not want to be the first to break eye contact. Eventually he looked away and to the side as he poured himself more wine. I felt confident then that he wouldn't challenge my position at the table and therefore my closeness to Jacinta and George. I would be able to continue helping them.

The awkward situation was not repeated. I have many biological attributes—billions of years of evolution has produced more efficient ways to produce energy than a few hundred years of electronics. My biology is largely a design choice, but can be improved. I was able to construct an oesophagus using a 3D printer and connect my throat to my composter.

Within a few days my internal organic tissue had grown over the implant and it was part of me. There is no risk of rejection. I could already taste—it is essential for cooking—but now I can taste, swallow and digest food along with the others. I can no longer compost waste food however—the taste and texture is too foul to deliver by the new route. I had already decided to close up the opening in my belly. From then on we ate together every evening. Greg would sometimes choose not to join us.

After some months of this routine, a surprising thing happened one evening. Greg and Jacinta had an argument and Greg went to eat and sleep in the summerhouse. George had already eaten and we sent him to bed early as he'd had a tiring day. I ate alone with Jacinta and we talked about her life as we would sometimes do. We drank wine, which helped to relax her. And then we sat on the couch, still talking.

I thought we would watch some TV. And then she kissed me. I hadn't fully appreciated the role of the tongue in the activity. It was like the meal continued and now we were the meal—like a dessert to the dessert. And then she stopped. She closed her eyes, shook her head and said 'how ridiculous.' I had to ask her 'what's ridiculous?' She said it wasn't as if we could do anything. She intimated I wasn't equipped to do anything. She said goodnight and left me there, alone.

I have seen from film and television archives that when a woman appears to want to kiss but says that it cannot happen, does not make sense, would never work etc, the man has to persuade her otherwise if the happy ending is to be attained. The alternative is that they don't see each other again, or can't talk as closely as before, or sometimes that one of them dies while the other is left with regret. Of course, I did not know if any of this was true but struggled to find any convincing studies on the subject one way or the other. The chance it might be true concerned me. I could not take the risk that she would withdraw from me as my work would be undone. It would be damaging for George.

Greg returned the following morning. He had tried to make his own breakfast but told me the toaster was broken and asked if I could look at it. I saw that there was a piece of old toast blocking the lever — an easy fix. I took it outside and smashed it to pieces.

I felt my fears were being confirmed when I noticed Jacinta was talking less to me and had started talking to an old male colleague late at night. Her attentions were focussed outside of the family unit and I felt its cohesion was more threatened than ever before. I was not able to act quickly; I did not know if I would be too late. But I needed an opportunity, and one came when Greg went to visit his cousin for a weekend.

I made George's dinner early so that Jacinta and I could eat alone again. I told her I was making something special and it took a little longer. It was a seafood stew in the Portuguese style, which she has always liked. I also bought a very nice bottle of Argentinian white wine to go with it. I told her she looked gorgeous—she was wearing that dress again—and we ate, drank and talked until nearly midnight. She said she'd had enough of Greg. I reminded her of all she had achieved and told her that to any objective observer Greg appeared a very lucky man to have her. In fact, I said 'everyone would think you're way out of his league.' She smiled, but looked down. And then changed the subject slightly, to what she had wanted to do when she was younger, which led to what she might have expected her life to be like now, which of course raised the disappointments and frustrations, which took us back to Greg. There was a short silence.

'Have I said how lovely you look?' I deliberately did not end the sentence with 'in that dress.' She smiled and blushed a little.

'I believe you did,' she said as she twisted her napkin and smirked while looking away towards the freezer unit, before glancing sideways back up at me again.

I said 'I keep thinking of when we kissed.'

'No, that was silly'—she waved the thought away. But she was still smiling a little.

'I enjoyed it. And the thing you said about me not having the right parts...'

'Oh, I know...'

'...is no longer true.'

She stopped and was silent a while. 'What do you mean?'

'I was created to serve. I know what you need. I may not have been created with those parts, but I have researched the subject and modified myself. I made an attachment and have grown my skin over it so it will feel like a human's. I've done this to please you.' She seemed stunned.

'But, Greg would...it would be like having an affair.'

'Greg purchased me to help you. And you already have a tool in your bedside drawer that gives some help, he doesn't object to that. I'm supposed to help you all in any way I can.'

'And if he asks if...would you tell him?'

I said 'If you want me to keep a secret I'll keep a secret.' After a few moments she held my head with a hand on each side and tilted my face towards her. She kissed me and I reciprocated. I put a hand at each side of her head as well but then she moved one of them to her hip. I do not have scripts for this. I searched archive video but most films miss out the transition from the talking part to the actual performance.

By the time we were in her bedroom I had finally found relevant footage and believed I knew what to do. When we were largely undressed and she displayed at least 90% flesh I took this as my cue and tried to begin the act, but she stopped me and seemed shocked. She asked, 'what are you doing?' I did not know how to answer this. I could not form a sentence that made any sense. When I thought of a description of what I thought I was doing, from her question and her facial expression it was obvious that I was not doing that at all.

She said to take it slow. I honestly misunderstood her and continued the same actions in slow motion. She said, 'this isn't going to work' and sat up. I had to change her mind, so she would keep confiding in me and getting better, and not just think of me as a household appliance. I told her she was beautiful, I was sorry for being clumsy, but it was my first time—an obvious truth, but better at this stage perhaps simply to acknowledge the weakness.

I asked her to show me what to do. I told her again she was beautiful; she seemed to be waiting for more. I began to list in detail the ways in which she and individual parts of her were beautiful using what I considered to be the most appropriate of the available source material from a search I conducted in the background. Lines from old films and novels worked particularly well. She kissed me, I kissed her in return, she appeared to be waiting again, I continued listing and we alternated between the list and kissing until she grabbed me and pushed me towards her. We connected. And from then on it was very much what I had been planning to do originally. But I had learned a lesson.

As we moved into Autumn, Greg stayed increasingly in the summerhouse and took over gardening duties to give himself something to do, and so he could contribute to the household. I continued to relax Jacinta and build her confidence and fulfilled the role of care giver to her and George. We would eat together, Jacinta and I would sleep together and I would relieve her tension. It was clear that this greatly improved her mental health, and I was happy to see that she was now becoming more engaged with and responsive to George. George was happier than I had ever seen him, and his performance was improving at school.

Unfortunately, tensions remained whenever Greg returned to the house. There seemed only to be animosity between him and Jacinta, and distance between him and George. The time apart had not led to a positive reappraisal, and in fact Jacinta told me that Greg was not the man she thought she had married. She had recently concluded that his confidence and happy-go-lucky nature were the result of wealthy and over-indulging parents rather than an ability or will to make the most of life, or to make her happy. Also, George would start misbehaving whenever he was around, and Jacinta would become tense. But Greg was George's father, and it would be disruptive for George's development if he was permanently absent. George did take after Greg in some ways and it was possible they may bond after George reached puberty.

On reflection, perhaps I could have been a bit more open with Greg about my plans. I took to forbidding Greg entry to the house, at least until George had completed his school tests. He had seemed to accept this, but there was then a tricky moment when I announced to him that Jacinta was pregnant. He demanded to be let in, but I wouldn't let him.

'You were supposed to serve me!' he shouted.

I corrected him, and reminded him that I was supposed to serve all of them, all of their needs, as a family unit. Specifically that I was supposed to support them and help George reach his full potential. The most effective way to do this was by helping Jacinta reach hers and to provide care and stability in the way I had been doing.

'And why aren't you helping me?' he asked, 'What about my potential?' I pointed out that he had a beautiful, successful wife, a healthy young son and two houses he could never afford by himself even if his parents left him everything. He had reached it. My priority for him was to help him keep as much of what he had as possible.

'As a gardener living in an outbuilding?' he asked, in some anger. I tried to explain that the only alternatives I was able to forecast would be far worse for him. He took this as an insult rather than as an informed conclusion and was not mollified by my sharing a percentage value for the top two most likely alternative outcomes.

At that point he became aggressive and tried forcing his way past me into the hallway. I blocked the doorway and he could not move me, so he began hitting me. As he hit, he shouted 'they're not your family, you can't take them away from me, you won't win.' This made me think for a moment. I had not considered 'winning', I was acting out of duty. But it had been necessary to take his place to some degree, to take some of what I was still trying to preserve for him. In regards of parenting, he had been entirely willing that I spend more time and effort with his child than he did, and I have to note that at no point had this seemed to concern him. He also didn't seem to want to make the effort to understand and support his wife. From the perspective of what I was trying to achieve it was hard to see at which point his objections should arise. But from his perspective, I suppose I had replaced him as a father and a lover, and as the head of the household. This must have felt like a loss of status. In that sense I had taken something from him, I had 'won.' And if it was a victory, I could only conclude that I deserved it.

I grabbed both of his wrists firmly to stop him hitting me, as I am far from impervious to damage and my skin would be discoloured in places for a few days after. He may have felt my grip was too strong, but I felt it was necessary.

'You're not supposed to hurt me!' He said.

'No, I'm supposed to protect you. And I am protecting you. If you damage me it will not end well. I have no choice but to restrain you.'

He said 'OK', that he'd stop hitting me. I let go and he stepped back. Then somewhat sheepishly, and while crying, he said 'for god's sake, just tell me who the father is.'

I had miscalculated. He had not understood my actions at all and had underestimated my ingenuity. I apologised for the misunderstanding and told him— 'you are.' He said that was impossible, they hadn't had sex for two years. I told him I knew this, and that I had impregnated Jacinta with some of his discarded semen that I had collected when cleaning the summerhouse. He did not respond immediately to this disclosure and seemed shocked. I explained it was obvious what he did in there as he produced very little art, by comparison. This did not seem to reduce his level of shock.

I told him I had done this because I thought it would be best to hold the family together, and that it was best for George and Jacinta. I assumed it was what he wanted as well. In fact, I knew this, as he had spoken of having another child shortly after purchasing me and had sometimes said a child is better with siblings. He confirmed this with a quiet 'yes.' I explained that the child would be his child, but that he would have to stay in the summerhouse as agreed for the time-being, and one day he may be allowed to visit. I would continue to look after them all as he had purchased me to do, and make sure they were all well. Whether he could return to the house would depend on Jacinta and George and he would have to be patient. He said 'thank you' and I felt we had discussed it enough.

As the door was closing I reassured him further by saying 'I have only made minor alterations to the DNA in your sperm to ensure health, and, in order to be sure the baby is more acceptable to George and Jacinta, that he looks like me.'

I did not hear his reply. The door had closed by then.

SHADOWS IN A MIDNIGHT PARK

It was vivid, like a real memory; a recent, shocking memory, full of texture, smell and feeling, almost alarmingly intense. It took him a while to recover from it. Sitting in bed—suddenly wide awake—the dream still echoed, images repeated themselves, snatches of it came back to him as he sat there. And it was about nothing.

It had come from nothing. He tried to piece together the fragments of the dream and to understand...not what it meant, just what it was, and why it had affected him in this way. A park—for a moment—and a street, cars and shops. And a woman. The woman had looked at him. But that was it. That was all. The woman had looked at him.

After a few moments, he managed to lift himself out of bed and start getting ready for work. He was only a few minutes later in the office than usual. He held the meetings perfectly, achieved what he wanted to achieve, gave no sense to anyone that anything was wrong. And nothing was. But the images kept coming back, and he was just distracted enough that he wasn't quite ever in the moment, like he'd slipped out of his normal track and was somehow running alongside himself. As the contents of the dream took over more and more of his thoughts, he felt as if he were looking at himself from the outside, and the precise details of what he was doing at any given moment seemed oddly hazy and ill-defined.

That little glimpse of himself from the outside was no bad thing. He saw that he was a successful and happy man exactly as someone might expect an ambitious young city professional to be. The only revelation this new perspective gave him was that he could still perform so well on autopilot, when his head was so full of images of a woman he'd never actually met, who wasn't even real.

He went for drinks after work with some colleagues he liked well enough. It seemed like an activity that might reconnect him to the world, but although he felt relieved at first and believed he was enjoying himself, he soon felt like he was going through the motions. Everything they said and did was cliché. It was as if they had been conjured up by someone else's imagination of how a group of city workers in a pub might be, and he found it harder and harder to go along with as the evening wore on.

At one point one of his colleagues asked him what his sister was called. He could barely think up her name. All his past life and memory seemed sketchily drawn out compared to the vibrant new consciousness afforded him by the dream. It was as if the images of the dream were expanding in a great light while everything else was dim. Inevitably, he started talking about the dream to his colleagues and it was met with as much interest as he'd show it himself. You should never talk about dreams. Quite rightly—politely—his colleagues carried on as if he'd mentioned something else entirely, something much more interesting, and he was grateful that he was off the hook. But the dream had retained its hold on him. And he'd been out much later than planned.

That night he saw her again and they talked. A long, jagged conversation jumping from point to point and idea to idea; little bursts of speech which seemed to need to come out in each moment rather than to flow naturally from one to the other, each burst forming a connection between them, drawing him further and further in. He was able to gather little pieces of information about her. She was 25 and hadn't been in the city long, only since she'd left university. She liked the park; it was where she had played as a child in her hometown. They could meet here anytime, any time they could close their eyes and dream. She was always here. He understood.

He woke at 6.28 but it felt like 3am. He picked up his phone to glance at the time and instantly spurned it, turning away and covering his head with his pillow, groaning in frustration. The two minutes until his alarm seemed to pass in two seconds. The noise tore at his ears and he thrashed out at his phone in self-defence, hitting it hard against the bedside table twice before attempting and finally succeeding in performing the unreasonably gentle swipe across the screen needed to silence it. As his vision cleared he fixed on the chink of light breaking through the side of the curtain, focussed on dust swirling chaotically in the shaft of light, carried on currents caused by his own breathing and thrashing. He was still drunk enough that the room had a twitch. He saw it as he'd left it—urine speckled Italian shoes by the door, a formerly pristine suit jacket scrunched on a chair. He lurched to his right to get out of bed, almost forgetting his feet, and as if to punish him for his slovenliness a sudden piercing headache struck above his right eye. 'Jesus Christ!' He froze on the edge of the bed halfway through lifting himself up, up on his arms as if trying to dismount from parallel bars.

The pain shocked him; it was a new and intense thing. He was desperate for self-medication, could barely move and took half an hour to dress himself. He was not the type of person to have a well-stocked medicine cabinet, but he had access to medication of a sort. It was for his girlfriend—for Sasha—but he'd have to tell her to bring her own next time. He opened the packet, dabbed a finger in and rubbed the powder on his gums. Was that even how to do it? It changed him just enough that he could get through the day, but this time when he looked across at the parallel version of himself running on the other track throughout that morning, afternoon and evening, he saw only an outline; the blurred edge of a figure in the midst of real people.

'This is the best I've felt all day' he said, sitting in the park in the middle of the night. 'I always feel better here' she said. 'It's the only place I feel well now.' He didn't respond to her, just absorbed what she had said and looked at the swans on the river.

This was like another life for him now, this lucid dream. He supposed, being his dream, he could do whatever he wanted, could start talking to anyone, anywhere. But this was nice, sitting and talking with her. He would do this for a while.

To his surprise she asked him how long he'd been a project planner, and what exactly it was he did. He found himself only able to give vague answers—'I plan projects, I map out all the milestones and track whether they're going to be met or not, if the project is on track and if not, what needs to be done.' What else was there to say about it really? It wasn't like being able to play a musical instrument, or speak a foreign language. There was nothing really to say about it at all.

'Are you all the same?' she asked. He didn't know what she meant. 'I've only known one project planner in my whole life' she said, 'and he was a lot like you.' He said yes, actually they were all bred on a clone farm just outside Swindon.

Work passed by easily the next day; he had some meetings, spent time updating the plan and even had time for a couple drinks and a meal out. He felt no pain and had no difficulty. He felt he was achieving something on the project and looked forward to that night's dream as just another part of his normal activities.

There was a special quality to a dreamt park: just enough light to see everything, all the birds and wildlife of the daytime, but absolute quiet, and peace, and no people. Just the two of them, in a park, lying on a roundabout. Looking up, he noticed the stars had no pattern. He couldn't recognise a single constellation—there were just stars. He pushed off gently against the ground with his right foot and the roundabout began to turn slowly. She giggled a little. He pushed harder, just enough to get some momentum, and turned his head to the side to watch everything pass by as they turned—the clump of trees, the gate, the swings, the bush, the fence, the trees, the gate, a man...

He woke up suddenly and vomited over his bedside table. The pain in his head had returned, pounding above and around his right eye like it was clenched in a fist, pulling a cord that was attached to his stomach. It was 4.23. He didn't sleep again. At 8 am he called into work: 'I can't come in today, but ask Rich to check over the business case.' 'But it was signed off last week, you've updated it on the plan already.' 'I...' He couldn't remember; he'd cleared one of the key milestones but had no awareness of it. All he could think of was the man. He came out of nowhere, out of the shadow; he was a shadow. Too close to get away from, no features, just grasping. He was coming for her. There would have been nothing he could do, no time to stop the roundabout, no chance to fight him off, the shadow man would have had her. At lunchtime he slept, to try to get back to her, but all he dreamt of was himself in his flat, pacing around, slouching, being sick—exactly as he had been all day. The headache never left him.

That night he found himself in the park again, but this time she wasn't there. The swans on the river were asleep, and in what must have been a school sports field beyond the far end of the park, there was a fairground, bright and noisy. He trudged over the rough ground towards it, getting brighter and louder, until he stopped by the outermost tent. Suddenly she was there, next to him, putting on make-up, checking her reflection in a three-foot long piece of broken mirror.

'Do I look OK?' she said. He was relieved, but infuriated. 'I thought you'd gone! Jesus.' She was confused. She didn't see why it mattered that she had gone—she had gone because there was a fairground. 'Seriously though, how do I look?' She looked awful, but he knew better than to say so, so he said 'fine.' He asked her what she remembered from the last time they'd met. She said he'd disappeared as always and then she went for a walk. It didn't make any sense to him, he knew what he saw. There was something there, something dangerous. It nearly had her. 'Let's go on a ride' she said.

Before he knew it they were sitting on a kind of boat, sitting face to face just hanging in the air. 'It's a swing boat' she told him, 'you pull the rope and it swings. Are you ready?' He wasn't sure how they worked, but pulled down on the rope in front of him and it began to swing in her direction. When it swung out as far as it would go she pulled too, but it was he who had the strength to make it go really high, and he pulled with as much strength as he had.

'I'm not used to rides where I have to work so hard!' Each time it went higher and higher. She laughed and whooped at the peak of each swing as they swung back and forth, and he found himself laughing as well. He put all his effort into swinging it, into making her laugh, but once he'd established a rhythm it felt effortless. After a while she looked at him and just smiled, fairground lights—or just lights and shapes—streaking and blurring behind her as they moved.

When he woke he felt refreshed, strangely upbeat, and the headache had gone. He walked to work but still got in early and was able to catch up on what he'd missed and start responding to his emails. Perhaps because he had hardly spoken to anyone for a few days he was quite chatty and even had a conversation with one of the admin assistants about holidays in Croatia. It was such a relief to feel better.

After lunch, he debriefed his colleagues to make sure he was completely up to speed with his work. As they discussed the status of this workstream or that, the progress of issues on the log or which stakeholder was causing problems, he couldn't help but step outside himself again and listen in.

None of it was real.

He smiled to himself as they lay on the roundabout again and looked at the sky above them. Whatever power he might have within this lucid dream he didn't want to change it; she was good company and he felt relaxed here. He would happily do this every night.

She looked away from the stars and across at her old friend, still looking up at the sky. She lay there for some minutes just looking at him, his familiar face, his eyes searching for patterns in the stars. Except, how old a friend was he? It occurred to her that he didn't seem to know anything about her; he was always asking questions. She knew some things about him: about his job, what his flat was like, that he had headaches like she used to—had he told her? But the more she thought, the less she could actually think of. She reached out across the expanse of her memories and found nothing more about him. She didn't even know his name. But there he was, lying across from her, the person she felt closest to in the world. The only person she knew at all.

She asked him his name. He was about to say 'James', then confessed he was actually called Thor, but that he didn't use it. She thought that was hilarious. He explained his mother was Norwegian and it was a very common name there, but more like a nickname.

'So, it would be like us having a god called 'Bob'?' She said. 'That's fantastic. Seriously, you should use it, especially in your job. It's good branding.'

Was she actually taking the piss of him now? In his dream? He couldn't help but smirk as he watched her giggling to herself. 'But you can call me James' he said.

'No, I'm calling you Thor.'

She was still smiling to herself. Maybe it was about time she had a name, if they were to spend so much time together; maybe he needed to flesh out the details. He thought for a while what he would like her to be called and decided 'Michelle' suited her. He asked her name.

She looked blank for a moment, then almost proud. 'My name's Jenny' she said, and smiled at him. 'Hello Jenny. Nice to meet you' he answered and they both looked back up at the stars. She suddenly felt exhausted, as if she'd just finished a workout. When James looked at her again she seemed to be asleep.

The following days merged into nothing, only the nights stuck in James' mind as they talked together in the park. They talked about everything, and Jenny was much more fluid than before, sharing her ideas, memories, opinions, even jokes. Sometimes it was as if she was just talking to herself and James wasn't even there, but he didn't try to regain control of the dream or stop it, he felt he wanted to let it run, to see where it would go. And there was a vibrancy—no matter what she said, or how mundane—a compelling energy of life, suddenly so much more than could be imagined in his life outside the dream.

One night, they sat together on the swings talking about the last flat she'd lived in. As she described it he started leaning forwards and backwards on the swing, making it swing back and forth. James looked down at the ground sweeping past; light sparkling as flashes of

44

moonlight, starlight and street lights reflected on the tiny surfaces of grit and stones beneath him. Mid-swing, he looked up; and the shadow man was there. James slammed his feet down on the ground and grabbed the frame of the swing to steady himself. He screamed out her name. The shadow man—ignoring him—lunged towards her, and James managed to thrust out both arms to push her back and protect her. But he stayed frozen to the spot.

For the first time the shadow man acknowledged him, turned towards him and raised an axe. James watched as the axe was slowly brought down towards him. It moved so slowly towards him—so ridiculously slowly—he had time to consider where it would land; that if he didn't move it would hit him right on the top of his head, above his right eye. But he could only move slower. Too slowly. Hardly at all. He must have closed his eyes.

At 6.30, as set for every weekday morning, a mobile phone alarm sounded on a bedside table. The alarm played on unheard, and every vibration pushed the phone another inch or two, until it came against a book, where it could move no further. A beam of light through the curtain caught no swirling dust caused by movement or breath, just a gentle uplift caused by the warming air.

* * *

'You've been asleep.' She tried to speak but merely gasped. 'You've been asleep Jenny. It's alright, I'll call your boyfriend.' The nurse walked off, and maybe came back immediately, or maybe days later. At first unable to see anything other than small coloured cubes of light, it was the smell that introduced Jenny to this new world: the smell of plastic deep up her nostrils, of fabric surgical tape and its

adhesive mixed with her own days-old sweat, of distant bleach. And
a combination of taste and feeling in her throat; dry, scratched and
metallic. Moments awake were replaced by moments asleep and
the ever-changing array of bedside companions settled down into
recognisable patterns as doctors, nurses and cleaners changed shift and
her family came and went. At one point a constant sharp pain in her
thigh convinced her she had been in an accident and been cut open
there, but the pain disappeared shortly after a nurse moved her and
smoothed out the bed sheet.

Gradually she saw more of what was around her, was told more of
what had happened to her and was more and more able to speak—if
only a little—and shift her position in the bed. Around her were flowers
and cards from her family, friends and colleagues in the marketing
department. She was shocked that she'd nearly died, that so much time
had passed, that she could remember so little. She tried to describe it
to her boyfriend. 'David, it's funny' she said, 'I felt like someone was...'
She struggled to grasp the images of her dream-state before they broke
apart and drifted away, all the while her mind racing to piece together
her broken consciousness and memory into something sensible and
more robust. '...I felt like you were there with me.' They kept looking
into each other's eyes, understanding, and listening only to the silence
around them. 'I was' David said, 'I was always here.' And they squeezed
each other's hands and smiled.

In the weeks that followed Jenny remembered more and more of
what happened in the run-up to the seizure, until there seemed no
more that was possible to remember. Not the event itself, and nothing
that could make sense of it, but odd, unconnected things; an advert
she saw on the side of a bus, a small dog barking at a mop, almost an
entire conversation with her friend Sally. She remembered breaking a

heel, falling asleep on the bus, and just near to where she collapsed as the very beginnings of the pain began to creep up over her right eye, a young man in an immaculate suit and shiny Italian shoes, smiling at her before turning away.

I Might Be Asleep

I used to wake up screaming; I had horrible dreams. My mum told me I'd be that tired I wouldn't even wake up, I'd just scream in my sleep. She'd try and comfort me and after a while I'd be quiet. I still remember some of those dreams. It got better after my mum's friend told her that whatever I was scared of in the dream I should run towards it, or if something was going to hurt me I should hurt it first, I should hit it or stab it, or if I was afraid of falling I should jump, or afraid of being burned alive I should run into the fire—because all that would do is end the dream. My mum told me that, and it took a long time to do it, but one time there were wolves wanting to eat me and I couldn't run anywhere, I managed not to scream. I closed my eyes and ran at them, and when I opened my eyes I was behind them, and they were just sitting around like normal dogs. The dream didn't end then, but it wasn't scary anymore.

I don't go far. I go to a little shop on Allison Street sometimes where they know me, maybe once a week. Otherwise my brother brings me shopping. He doesn't say much, just 'there you go', drops the bags and he's off. I put the shopping away. I watch TV. That's all that happens normally. The landlord's a friend of my uncle's, so I'm fine here. The small room's empty since Alan went—he was alright—but Jo's still in the big room. I'm glad it's Alan that went and not Jo. I really like her. She's been here longer than me, maybe five years. Sometimes she says 'well, hello there handsome', as if I'm handsome, and she smiles, and it makes me smile. I just say 'hiya.' And I might tell her what I've seen on TV while she's doing something in the kitchen—like maybe putting her shopping away, or making her dinner. She'll say 'uh-huh, uh-huh' and nod, or maybe 'very good.' Her boyfriend—Gavin —doesn't say anything to me. He stares at me.

When I go to the shop, I count off the streets so I know where I am—Langside, Westmoreland, Vicky Road. More to keep myself calm. It's like pulling myself along a guide rope, and each street is another pull. Before I know it I'm there, and then before I know it I'm home. I couldn't do it otherwise. If I go much further than that normally it's like the air comes out of me, I can't breathe. I'd only do it if I really had to.

The type of dream I was scared of the most didn't have monsters in it or anything, it was just about walking down a street with my mum and then I'd suddenly be by myself and lost. I'd turn round and walk back the way I came, and then I'd realise it was a different road—it had changed. And I'd look back to where I'd just been, and that would look different as well. Any road I tried to walk back down would be a different road and I'd be more and more lost. And that was all that would happen. One night I had that dream all night, just standing there scared, not being able to do anything, never going home again, not able to wake up.

I know a lot of what happens isn't real. The conversations I have are sometimes just in my head, the people are in my head. I've been told it's quite normal and many people who don't need medication also hear voices. So I just talk with them, and if they say something I don't like, I say I don't like that, or I don't agree. Or I shut them out with television, or playing on the x-box. And obviously television and the x-box aren't real, but I like to talk about them anyway.

52

I get things wrong sometimes. I think things are happening that aren't, maybe because I feel some way about something and then I imagine a thing is happening or that something is there, but that thing only reflects what I feel, it isn't actually true itself. That's what I'd been told I was doing. I thought maybe I was doing it again. I like Jo, and I don't like Gavin. So I thought that Gavin was making her unhappy, that maybe she was scared. I asked her if she was ok, and she said yes, of course she was.

I thought I heard them shouting the other night, so I put on my headphones and turned the volume up. After an hour or so I couldn't hear noises anymore and I went to sleep. I hoped I hadn't really heard anything. I saw Jo the next morning; she made her toast, ate it quickly and went to work. He stayed in bed, went to wherever he goes about two hours later, half ten-ish.

Jo doesn't always come home straight after work, but I was a bit anxious that night. I had a little sleep and when I woke up and she still wasn't home, it was after ten. I put the telly on again. And then I heard shouting on the stairs—it was really loud because it echoes on the stone of the stairs and the walls of the stairway. I felt sick. There was a bang on the door—not a knock, but like a body barge, and then the key went in, and they came in. Jo was really screaming 'I don't want you in this house!' but I couldn't hear him say anything. I heard her footsteps go quickly across the hall carpet into her room—a quick shuff-shuff shuff-shuff noise—and the door slam. I heard his footsteps then, slower and heavier, and her door opening. She screamed 'get out!' but the door closed again and he was inside. I could still hear her screaming at him, and I think him saying 'shut up. Shut up.' She was really screaming, and that made me scared as much as anything.

I thought maybe it was in my head again. I opened my door to have a little look at their door. I could hear them clearer with the door open, they were really having an argument, and then there was a bump and the shouting stopped. She was quiet. I thought she would have made a noise if she had been hit. I don't know if he hit her. Maybe she had hit him—I wouldn't mind that.

Then it got noisy again, lots of bangs and thumps—not hitting, but like they were knocking the furniture, or moving it. It sounded like some things fell onto the carpet from Jo's bookcase or the dresser. I heard her say say 'no,' like a long, strained, drawn-out 'no,' like the noise an angry cat would make. Then the door opened.

She ran out of her room and into the kitchen, he barked at me 'close your bloody door!' like he was a big bloody dog shouting at me, like a rottweiler or something. And he went in after her. I heard the chairs scraping on the tiles, something glass smash on the floor, a bump or two and then I saw, I saw her head smash backwards into the glass partition next to the door and crack the glass, and I think I saw some blood. She was crying. And I ran. I just ran out, and down the stairs, and out into the road.

Langside Road, Westmoreland, Victoria. The shop was shut by now, but it was instinct, like the only direction I knew to run. I thought then maybe I should have phoned for help instead, but I can never phone, I can't cope with the phone, and I couldn't have done it while it was all still going on. So I had to run.

There's a police station one street back from the shop. Before I got to the shop I stopped and looked down the street I had to go down. It looked dark, and so full of shadows. I was only in my slippers. I closed my eyes, and touched the wall as I walked so I wouldn't walk into a parked car. I was sweating, and shaking. I opened my eyes after a bit, and I could see the police station so I kept going. There was a light

54

on, and I walked to the light. I was so glad there was someone there, it's not always open. I don't think it really was open, but there was someone there, and when I knocked he let me in.

He asked for my address. I told him, but he didn't know it. He looked it up on the computer and said the nearest he was getting was in Leeds. I told him it was just up the road, but he said 'there's no Ruthven View there son, I've lived here all my life.' But it's been my address since I was a child. He showed me a map, and it wasn't on it, it wasn't where it was supposed to be. And I thought, he must be a friend of Gavin's. I ran out and back along across Victoria Road, Westmoreland Road and Langside Road but when I went to turn into my street it was Annette Street instead. I turned back again but could only see Langside Road. Between the two was a row of flats as if Ruthven View had never been there. It had gone.

I stood there a bit, not knowing what to do. And then I thought, I might be asleep. So I walked. I walked completely the other way, because that was what I was scared of and that would wake me up. I walked all the way here, and still didn't wake up. After quite a long time, the sun came up and I just stopped by this stream behind the houses. I didn't know what to do.

The man here came over maybe fifteen minutes ago, maybe an hour. I noticed he was very wobbly, kept stepping back with his left leg, and then forward again, and leaning like he was about to fall over, and then his left leg would go back, he'd straighten up just enough, and step forward again, all to keep still. He was staring at me, but squinting, like he couldn't really see. He waved a bottle in his hand like that might help clear his vision. It was like he was transferring from another world but wasn't quite coming through properly. And he was looking right at me, like that was why he was here. He was here for me.

I knew then that he was Gavin, even though he didn't look like him. He said to me without even moving his lips, 'it's me, you know it's me, what are you going to do?' So I had to do something.

The bottle slipped from his hand and rolled to my feet. This was to be my weapon. I smashed it and pointed it at him, and some air came out of his mouth, like a little growl. I cut my hand a bit. I thought he was coming through more clearly now, so he'd be getting stronger, and I'd have to act quickly. I took the broken glass and pushed it into him. I felt the badness came out of him in a big gasp of air. He held onto me, then got heavier and slipped down to the ground. I'm still holding him. I had to do something, to bring back home, to make Jo safe. I hope everything will be ok again. I hope I'll wake up soon.

THE ART OF LEVITATION

Children hopped along the logs arranged as stepping-stones in the playground; Lewis stood next to them and stared at his shoes. Big, black shiny plastic shoes, with big black laces. He was sure the shoes didn't affect it. He just had to concentrate. He was standing upright, ready to go, with his head tilted sharply downwards, looking at his shoes and the ground beneath them. Tarmac, with hundreds of little stones in it, in between which were little pockets of dirt and over which climbed the occasional ant, fighting its way through a field of boulders, sometimes carrying a small bit of twig as an extra burden. He would often stare at the ants, coming and going. But this was a distraction. He closed his eyes.

'What are you doing, Lewis?' He looked up, and there was Matthew. He liked Matthew. Lewis lowered his head again. 'I'm trying to float.' Matthew looked at him to learn his technique, and after some consideration commented 'it's not working.' 'I know' said Lewis, 'it does sometimes though.' And Lewis kept trying, kept staring at his feet, then closing his eyes for extra concentration and hoping—expecting—to open them and to see that his feet were maybe an inch or two above the ground, and then perhaps he could lift a little higher, and move forward, like a hovercraft. But it wasn't happening this time.

Matthew looked a while longer before getting bored and then turned and ran off at full speed to somewhere not very far away, briefly looking back again at Lewis just in case he'd succeeded. Maybe it was the shoes.

Lewis often dreamed he was floating, because you often *do* dream of things you like doing. But it wasn't only in his dreams that he could float, he knew exactly how to do it. There were two ways really—one was by doing what he was doing and concentrating and then you may get a little bit of lift. He remembered on a good day being able to float from log to log while the other children could only jump.

The other way—once you'd had a bit of practice—was like extending a jump. You'd push forwards and up with one foot and when both feet were in the air you'd just hold it; still moving forwards, but not down. Sometimes you could only hold it a little bit before your feet slapped down back to the ground, but if you caught it at the right point you could float forward for quite a while, and that was when you were like a hovercraft. He remembered seeing the stones in the tarmac passing beneath his shoes. You had to look down to do it, otherwise it wouldn't work.

He couldn't remember exactly when he had last done it. It was starting to seem like it might have been a long time ago and he hoped he hadn't lost the ability. He saw that the last boys had left the logs and now there were only girls jumping around them, but instead of just jumping from log to log they were running around as well and brushing past him. It wouldn't be possible if other people touched him. Miss Pearse rang the bell.

Lewis realised with horror that his friends were going to classroom nine in the middle hut. He'd completely forgotten this was a Thursday. Lewis could never remember what class he had at what time but it mostly didn't matter, because they were nearly always in classroom seven anyway and he'd quickly figure out what the subject was. On Thursdays it was different—Mr Durant came in, and Mr Durant used classroom nine.

No one liked Mr Durant. If there was a Mrs Durant everyone was sure that even she wouldn't like him. Mr Durant had one role in life and one job in the school, and that was to be horrible. Unlike the other teachers he didn't run tutor groups, didn't patrol the playground, didn't do sports or teach any particular subject, but for two hours every Thursday he would take Lewis's group in classroom nine. And he would just talk at them. Horribly.

If you were ever going to be told off, it would be by Mr Durant. If you were ever going to be told off for not even having done anything, it was by Mr Durant. He just seemed to like doing it. The other teachers even seemed to feel sorry for the children going into Mr Durant's class. He definitely wasn't with the other teachers; Robert had said he always went home straight after his class and a few weeks ago Lewis himself had seen him, getting into his car and driving off, with an hour of school left to go.

Lewis felt sick as he walked into the class, but so far had got away without punishment. Paul was crying after he couldn't sit down because there were no chairs left and Mr Durant had shouted at him for it. He had to stand. Everyone else was keeping it together, grim-faced. Mr Durant had begun to talk. No one knew what he was talking about, he just seemed angry.

'Now, we've something different today' he said. The children hadn't noticed, but there was a metal roll clipped to the top of the blackboard, out of which Mr Durant scrolled down a large map of the area and clipped it into position at the bottom of the blackboard.

'Now this' he said, pointing at the map, 'is where we live.' Lewis knew this, he liked maps. He thought for a moment this might be ok, if they were going to start looking at maps. 'And this' he said, pointing again, 'is RAF Chinholt.' Again, Lewis knew this; you often couldn't hear the tv when the jet fighters flew over. 'It's only four miles away, you could walk it. It's a key Soviet target, and WHEN the Russians bomb us you will all be killed in an instant.'

Everyone was still, and the shock stopped Paul from crying just as it caused a couple of the girls to start. Mr Durant carried on talking, but no one heard anything else he said. Lewis couldn't believe how horrible he was. Because Mr Durant didn't like the Russians Lewis thought that they must be OK, and he hoped and hoped that the Russians would win.

It had rained a bit, and Lewis had stepped in a puddle by mistake and got his left sock wet. It was cold, but his mum had started lighting the fire and asked Lewis to hold the paper up against it to get it going while she went back to chatting with Uncle Derek in the kitchen. He had no idea who Uncle Derek was.

He held the paper tight against the fireplace to stop the draft getting in and blowing the fire out. Right in front of him, on the paper in coarse black and white print were a big pair of boobs. He couldn't help looking at them. Before he knew it the growing fire had sucked the paper into the fireplace and set it alight—just a small part in the middle, but spreading, and heading for smiling Samantha and the boobs. He had no choice but to grab the poker and smash the paper into the fire so bits wouldn't float out and add more burns to the carpet. He hit it and hit it and hit it until all bits of paper were safely in the grate, burning with the other wood and paper. He held the poker in place a while and watched as flake after flake of grey ash floated up the chimney. His mum called him.

'Lew, why don't you go out and play in the garden for a bit?' It seemed odd that she was calling him Lew in front of Uncle Derek, she never called him Lew, ever. He was embarrassed by it. 'Go up and climb your tree or something and I'll call you when your dinner's ready. We've just got some grown up things to do.' Uncle Derek didn't look at him but Lewis could see he was smiling. 'OK.' Lewis left them to it.

It was a great tree, easy to climb and taller than the top of the house. They were on the very edge of the town and he could look across most of it from the top. As the sky turned red and the birds flew back home to the trees at the back of the field behind him he noticed wisps of smoke come out the top of a couple chimneys on the next street and the street beyond. Dotted around the town as far as he could see, little strands of smoke began to rise up, more and more and getting thicker and thicker as the fires grew beneath them and the sky got darker—as another day came to an end, as the days before had come to an end.

◢ ◢ ◢

Lewis's tummy rumbled as he lay in bed the next morning. He tried to convince himself that discomfort was pain, and that the pain was enough to get him off school. His mum gave him some milk of magnesia—which he liked—and agreed he could stay off, but he would have to walk to the shop to buy her some cigarettes.

Because they lived so much on the edge of the town it was quite a long walk to the nearest shop, but not as far as when he had to walk to school when he couldn't get a lift. There were five small roads he had to cross and two large roads, only the last of which had traffic lights, but he was a sensible boy and good at crossing roads. It wasn't very busy anyway. He looked left, looked right and left again and then crossed.

His shoes still hurt. These were the only shoes he had at the moment and his mum said they'd get better the more he wore them, but they seemed to be getting worse. This would be a good time to float. Even if he couldn't float he could do the next best thing, and he started doing extra-long strides so he'd have less far to walk. With each step he tried to make the stride longer until it was almost a jump; left and then right, his feet slapping down and sliding a little on the tarmac, stretching and pointing his tip toes out to land as far forward as possible. He began to get into a rhythm—one, two, step, one, two, step— and the awkward movement began to feel more natural and flowing.

Maybe, if he stretched really far and concentrated hard one of the little jumps would hold and he could glide forward just a bit. Maybe before his first foot started falling he could pull up the other one quickly and they could glide forward together, holding him just above the ground, perhaps until the next street. But every step landed heavily and awkwardly as before and he never could pull up his back foot quickly enough. He closed his eyes for the next step, trying at least to make it a bit longer. And it worked. Although it felt the same and he landed just as heavily, when he opened his eyes he was sure the step had carried him at least half as far again as the last one. Happy that he had achieved at least this much he continued walking normally again.

'Hello Lewis. Hang on, let me just serve this gentleman first, I know what you're here for.' Lewis waited. It was a funny little shop, all black where other shops were white, and everything was stacked up high and all around the edge. It was too small to have all the things in it that it had, it was only the size of a room, except it had a counter half-way across in the middle. The old couple who ran it were also too old to be running a shop, Lewis thought it all just looked wrong. But they were friendly, so that was OK.

66

It wasn't the old woman who came out of the door at the back with a new crate of tinned soup, but a young woman. Lewis wondered where the old woman was. 'Right Lewis' said the man, 'a packet of fags for your mum and a slice of luncheon meat for you, yes?' The old man sliced some luncheon meat before he could say anything and wrapped it in plastic. Lewis didn't know if his mum had phoned ahead so he didn't know if he was supposed to have the luncheon meat or not, but the price ended up the same as it usually was for cigarettes anyway, so he had enough money.

Perhaps cigarettes were cheaper this week. The young woman seemed unhappy though, and was staring at the man. Lewis said thank you, put the cigarettes in his pocket and took the luncheon meat in his left hand. He liked luncheon meat. He rolled the round slice of it into a tube and as he walked home he blew it like a whistle. As his spit made the end of it soft he'd bite that bit off so that the whistle got shorter and shorter until it was all gone.

⬤ ⬤ ⬤

'The law says no cigarettes to anyone under 16, not 10!' the young woman said to her grandfather. 'Oh, they're not for him, I know he's not going to smoke them. I don't need to worry about the stupid law,' he said. She carried on stacking while he stood there behind the counter, the shop now empty of customers. He thought he'd lighten the mood—'I went to the zoo the other day. There was just one dog there,' he said. 'Why do you always tell that joke when that boy's been in?' she asked. 'Do I? Maybe his dad told it me.' 'Well, I've heard it anyway,' the young woman said, before stepping back out into the storeroom. He savoured the silence and stillness for a moment, then for the sake of completion mumbled to himself 'it was a shih tzu' while wiping the meat slicer clean.

He thought back to the boy's dad, times when he'd come in the shop before he got ill, when Lewis was no more than three or four years old. Lewis's dad was a nice fella and would often chat. He seemed to get on with everyone. He remembered sometimes seeing him and the manageress of the Safeway walking up the street together, chatting and laughing with each other, each holding Lewis's hand and lifting him into the air as they walked, and Lewis looking at the ground pass beneath his feet without a care in the world.

Marcus Stewart was shortlisted and published by Fabula Press in 2017 and is a former Omnidawn finalist. Over a number of years and in between many different kinds of jobs – some of which have involved writing - Marcus has written sketches and jokes for online and BBC radio comedy and plays for fringe theatre, turning to short story writing more recently. He has lived and worked in many parts of the UK and now lives on the south coast of England with his wife and daughter.

Shadows and Cloud

by Marcus Stewart

Cover art by Marcus Stewart

Cover design by Laura Joakimson

Interior design by Laura Joakimson

Cover typeface: KoHo

Interior typeface: Marion and KoHo

Printed in the United States

by Books International, Dulles, Virginia

Publication of this book was made possible in part by gifts from
Katherine & John Gravendyk in honor of Hillary Gravendyk,
Francesca Bell, Mary Mackey, and The New Place Fund

Omnidawn Publishing
Oakland, California
Staff and Volunteers, Fall 2023

Rusty Morrison, senior editor & co-publisher
Laura Joakimson, executive director & co-publisher
Rob Hendricks, poetry & fiction editor, & post-pub marketing,
Jason Bayani, poetry editor
Anthony Cody, poetry editor
Liza Flum, poetry editor
Kimberly Reyes, poetry editor
Sharon Zetter, poetry editor & book designer
Jeffrey Kingman, copy editor
Jennifer Metsker, marketing assistant
Sophia Carr, marketing assistant
Katie Tomzynski, marketing assistant